Five Naughty Kittens

A rhyming counting story

First published in 2004 by
Franklin Watts
338 Euston Road
London
NW1 3BH

Franklin Watts Australia
Level 17 / 207 Kent Street
Sydney
NSW 2000

A CIP catalogue record for this book is available
from the British Library.

ISBN 978 0 7496 5370 5

Series Editor: Jackie Hamley
Series Advisors: Dr Barrie Wade, Dr Hilary Minns
Series Designer: Peter Scoulding

Printed in China

Franklin Watts is a division of
Hachette Children's Books.

Five Naughty
Kittens

Written by
Martyn Beardsley

Illustrated by
Jacqueline East

W
FRANKLIN WATTS
LONDON•SYDNEY

Martyn Beardsley
"I love writing and reading stories. I like spooky stories best. I also like football and other sports. I hope you enjoy the book!"

Jacqueline East
"I have a puppy who is just as naughty as these kittens – he loves chasing frogs and eating my garden!"

Five naughty kittens
play in the drawer.

Oh no!

Now there are four!

Four naughty kittens
climb up the tree.

Oh no!

Now there are three!

Three naughty kittens
hide in the shoe.

Oh no!

Now there are two!

Two naughty kittens
stretch in the sun.

Oh no!

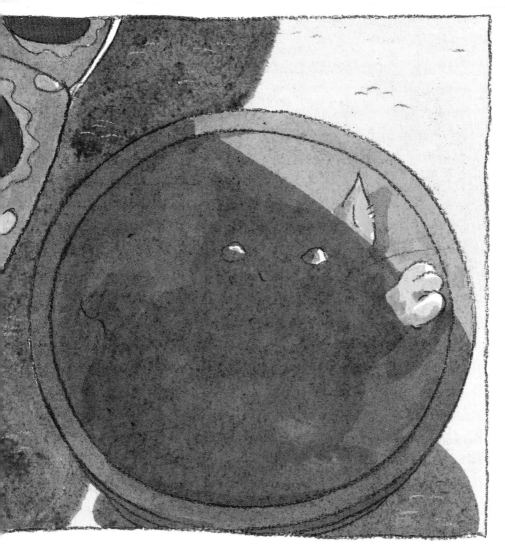

Now there's just one!

One lonely kitten
cries for the others.

21

Hurray! Back together,
sisters and brothers.

23

Notes for parents and teachers

READING CORNER has been structured to provide maximum support for new readers. The stories may be used by adults for sharing with young children. Primarily, however, the stories are designed for newly independent readers, whether they are reading these books in bed at night, or in the reading corner at school or in the library.

Starting to read alone can be a daunting prospect. READING CORNER helps by providing visual support and repeating words and phrases, while making reading enjoyable. These books will develop confidence in the new reader, and encourage a love of reading that will last a lifetime!

If you are reading this book with a child, here are a few tips:

1. Make reading fun! Choose a time to read when you and the child are relaxed and have time to share the story.

2. Encourage children to reread the story, and to retell the story in their own words, using the illustrations to remind them what has happened.

3. Give praise! Remember that small mistakes need not always be corrected.

READING CORNER covers three grades of early reading ability, with three levels at each grade. Each level has a certain number of words per story, indicated by the number of bars on the spine of the book, to allow you to choose the right book for a young reader:

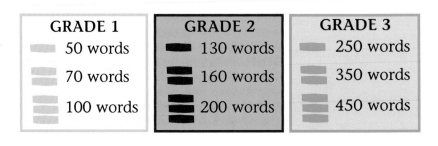

GRADE 1	GRADE 2	GRADE 3
50 words	130 words	250 words
70 words	160 words	350 words
100 words	200 words	450 words